Tumbler
and the Skate Park

Illustrations by Nigel Chilvers

EGMONT

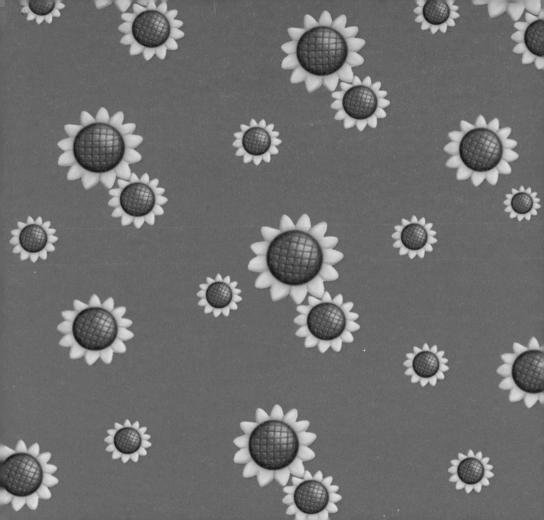

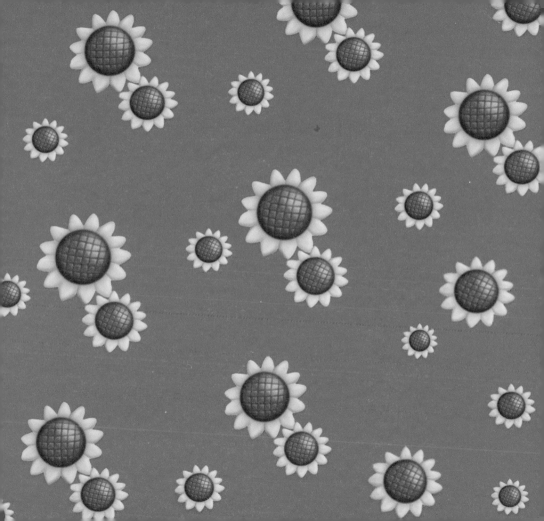

EGMONT

We bring stories to life

First published in Great Britain 2009 by Egmont UK Limited
The Yellow Building, 1 Nicholas Road, London W11 4AN

Endpapers and introductory illustrations by Craig Cameron.

HiT entertainment

ISBN 978 1 4052 4344 5

45939/2

Printed in Italy

FSC
www.fsc.org
MIX
Paper from
responsible sources
FSC® C018306

Egmont is passionate about helping to preserve the world's remaining ancient forests.
We only use paper from legal and sustainable forest sources.

This book is made from paper certified by the Forest Stewardship Council® (FSC®),
an organisation dedicated to promoting responsible management of forest resources.
For more information on the FSC, please visit www.fsc.org. To learn more about
Egmont's sustainable paper policy, please visit www.egmont.co.uk/ethical

When Tumbler the big mixer arrives to make cement for the skate park, his booming ways cause trouble. Will he learn that big doesn't always mean best?

"Right, everyone," said Wendy, one day. "We're building a skate park at Bobland Bay today – for all the skaters and skateboarders! It'll be big enough even for Scrambler to go on!"

"Wicked!" said Scrambler.

"Oh, dear! You'll need lots of cement then!" said Dizzy sadly, looking at her little mixer.

"Don't worry, Dizzy. Bob's bringing someone extra special to help," Wendy smiled.

Just then, Bob appeared. "Hi, everyone!" he called. "Meet the newest member of the team ... Tumbler!"

The machines all stared as a giant orange and green cement mixer rumbled up. "What a whopper!" they said together.

"I'm the biggest cement mixer you'll ever see! Nobody makes cement like me!" boasted Tumbler.

"Ha ha, I can believe that!" laughed Scoop.

Dizzy rolled up to Tumbler. "I'm Dizzy, I'm a cement mixer, too," she said, nervously.

"You don't look big enough to mix toothpaste! Ha, ha!" laughed Tumbler.

"Tumbler!" scolded Bob. "We thought Dizzy could show you around."

"If she can keep up on those tiny wheels!" laughed Tumbler, rudely.

"Follow me," said Dizzy, in a worried voice. And the two machines wheeled away.

The first stop on Dizzy's tour was Scarecrow Cottage. "This is Farmer Pickles' house," said Dizzy. "It's made of straw."

"Straw, eh? I suppose you were too little to make enough cement?" joked Tumbler.

"That's not true!" Dizzy replied crossly.

But Tumbler wasn't listening. He'd spotted Scruffty. "Hello, little doggie!" he boomed.

Poor Scruffty was so frightened of the big mixer, he disappeared into his kennel!

Meanwhile, Bob and the team were busy at the skate park site.

"Let's get digging!" said Muck, excitedly.

"Can we build it?" smiled Wendy.
"Yes, we can!" the machines replied.
"Er, yeah, I think so," added Lofty.

The machines began their work, but Bob was worried. "I hope Tumbler and Dizzy make friends," he said to Wendy.

"I'm sure Dizzy can handle him," she replied.

Next, Dizzy and Tumbler went to see Marjorie's house. Sunny and Carlo were playing outside on their rollerskates.

"Keep practising, kids!" said Tumbler loudly. "The skate park will be VERY BIG!"

But the children were startled by big Tumbler and they both fell over!

"You scared them!" said Dizzy, angrily.

"Sorry, wee one! I can't help being big!" Tumbler boomed to Dizzy. "Follow me!"

Dizzy raced after Tumbler but it was hard to keep up. "Wait for me!" she called. "Your wheels are bigger than mine!"

"And bigger is best!" Tumbler said. "Watch this! One load of my cement would take a little thing like you a week to mix!"

Tumbler's mixer began to rattle and rumble.

"Hey! You can't dump cement here!" huffed Dizzy. "You're just a big boaster!"

And off she rolled, leaving Tumbler behind.

Bob and the team had been very busy at the skate park. Sunny and Carlo came to have a look. "Wow!" they gasped.

"We've just got to pour the cement now," Bob told them. "I wonder where Dizzy and Tumbler have got to."

Seconds later, Dizzy arrived. But there was no sign of Tumbler. Bob and Wendy were puzzled.

"Er, I'll get him now!" said Dizzy, racing off.

In the woods, Tumbler was lost! "Hello? Is anyone th-th-there?" he cried. "Oh dear! I wish little Dizzy was here!"

Just then, Dizzy appeared! The clever little mixer had followed a trail of concrete dust.

"Dizzy! You found me!" Tumbler gasped. "I'm sorry I was rude."

"I may be small, but I know my way around!" she said firmly. "Now let's go, we've got cement to mix, and lots of it!"

Dizzy and Tumbler arrived at the site together, wheel to wheel.

"Sorry I'm late," said Tumbler, quietly.

"That's OK, Tumbler," Bob replied. "We need as much cement as you can mix!"

"Bob doesn't need me now," sighed Dizzy, looking at Tumbler.

"Silly Dizzy!" smiled Bob. "Tumbler's great for the big bits, but we need your cement to make the small things, like the benches."

Dizzy and Tumbler were delighted! The two mixers set to work straight away.

Tumbler poured his cement for the big bits and Dizzy did the little bits. They made a great team!

"Tumbler and Dizzy get on really well, don't they?" smiled Bob to Wendy.

Before long, their work was finished. The concrete needed to set before the skate park's grand opening, the next day.

Later, everyone gathered by the skate ramp to listen to Mr Bentley's speech. But before he could finish, Dizzy slipped down the ramp!

She whooshed down one side, and whizzed up the other, landing safely on all four wheels again. Everyone cheered!

"That was amazing, Dizzy! I'm way too big to do that!" gasped Tumbler.

"Ha, ha! Sometimes being little is just the right size!" Dizzy beamed.

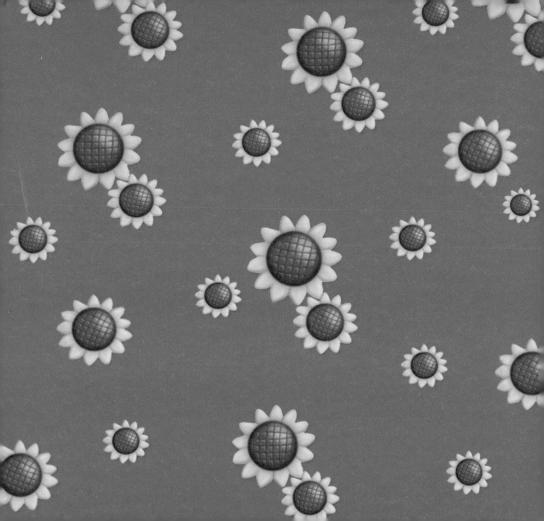

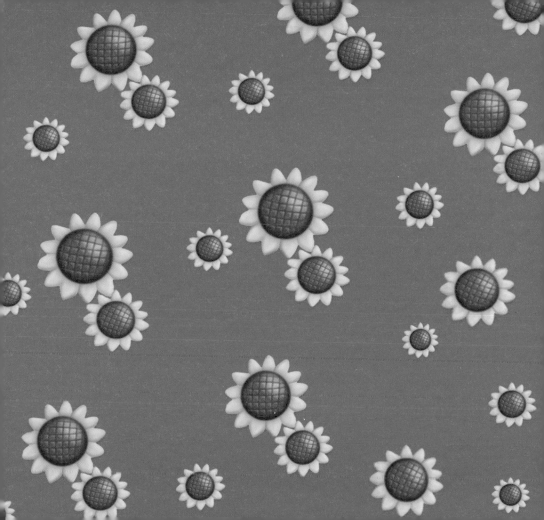

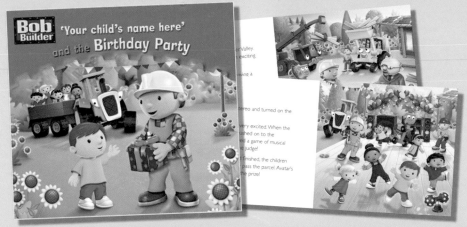